H. C Bispham

The Wonderful Stories of Fuz-Buz, the Fly, and Mother Grabem, the Spider

H. C Bispham

The Wonderful Stories of Fuz-Buz, the Fly, and Mother Grabem, the Spider

ISBN/EAN: 9783744707732

Printed in Europe, USA, Canada, Australia, Japan

Cover: Foto ©Andreas Hilbeck / pixelio.de

More available books at **www.hansebooks.com**

THE

WONDERFUL STORIES

OF

FUZ-BUZ THE FLY

AND

MOTHER GRABEM

THE

SPIDER.

PHILADELPHIA
J. B. LIPPINCOTT & CO.,
1867.

MRS. GRABEM AND FUZ-BUZ.

RS. GRABEM was a hairy spider who knit cobwebs and caught flies and brought up a small household of nine young spiders.

When I first knew this happy family, and learned all the wonderful things they heard and did, their home was as pretty a place as a spider need want. Their web was spun to and fro across the crotch of an old apple tree, and when they looked down they could see the green grass, and when they looked up they could see the great jolly red apples which must have looked to those young spiders just as the stars look to our own young folks.

On one side of their web, Mrs. Grabem had knit with great labour a long dark cave all of cobweb, where the family slept at night, and where they lay trembling while the great winds blew and the tree rocked and bent.

One fine breezy morning in June, when the leaves

above were clapping their palms for joy at growing, and when the birds were tossing little love songs to one another, the old lady sat mending her web which a great wasp had broken. Meanwhile, the young spiders chased each other along one thread and down another and shook the dew from the web as they played.

"Ah!" said the eldest of them, as he saw it sparkle in the sun, "these must be the diamonds we have heard about."

"No," said another, "they look to me blue, they are turquoises."

"Geese!" said a third, who was on a distant part of the web, "they are drops of gold, any one can see they are yellow."

At this they fell to abusing each other, when suddenly the old lady cried out, "Foolish children, if you change places you will see that each of you is right. You make me think of a tale which my grandmother used to tell me. It is a story which has come down in our family from your ancestor who gave Robert Bruce such very good advice without ever saying a word. You know that the king was looking at the spider when he was swinging a line, striving to fasten it. The spider having tried six times was about to stop, for before this spiders never tried more than six times. But when he looked up and saw the king he knew just what was needed to give him courage, and therefore it was that the spider made

one more mighty effort, and so at last made fast the
web.

"Thus you see that our ancestor invented trying seven
times, although I think the Bruce usually gets more credit
than the spider. When this wise spider grew older he
went to Spain in the helmet of the good Lord Douglas
who was killed by the Moors, so that they got his helmet
and your great-great-great-grandfather, who kept quiet
enough in the darkest corner until he was carried to
Granada, where he lived a long while and found the flies
many, and tender, and of good flavour. And this was one
of his stories which he had gotten at Granada, when he
lay among the Moors."

Then all the young spiders listened, and the old mother
spider began.

"One night the King Almanzor was walking alone
when he overheard three water-carriers gossiping.

"'I would not be the King,' said Amric, the first who
spoke. 'Every morning before prayers I peep through a
crack in the wall of the Palace garden, and always I see
the King grave and sober, just when the sun is rising
red and the birds are laughing and telling their dreams.
I would not be a King, to look sober at dawn every day
in the year. A grave man is the King.'

"'Bosh!' said the second, whose name was Hassan.
'The King is a sad man. He must have done some evil
in his youth, for just before noon-day prayers I look into

1 *

the Palace garden from my window, and lo! always the King kneels weeping at the great fountain, which we call the forest of waters.'

"'And I,' cried Amrah, 'think ye both wrong. A merry man is King Almanzor. For ever at evening, when the minarets call to prayer, I have seen the King at the fountain laughing, always laughing, always glad. A foolish man must the King be to laugh at nothing.'

"'He's too sober,' said one.

"'Too sad,' cried the second.

"'Too merry,' said the third.

"Then each held to his own opinion, and abused the others, until from words they came to blows.

"This roused the guard, who seized upon the whole three, and was taking them away, when the King whispered to the Captain to bring them to the Palace next day.

"Accordingly in the morning they were brought to the King in the garden before prayer time.

"'I hear,' said Almanzor, 'that you talked of me last night. It is said that you think me sober, sad, and foolish.'

"Not one of them answered.

"'I will think of your crime, and how you shall be punished. Begone, and return hither at noon.'

"At noon-tide they were brought again to the King,

who said to them gravely, 'You have abused the King. You shall die to-morrow.'

" 'Woe is me!" cried they all, and as they were led away the King stayed weeping by the water's edge.

"But at evening, the guard took them out yet once more, and this time the King was merry, and the sound of music mocked their sadness.

" 'You are pardoned,' said the King Almanzor. 'Judge not lightly of me again. In the morning I reflect on the crimes which I have to judge, and then I am grave. At noon I condemn some to die, and then ever I weep. But at night-fall I pardon the least guilty, and then always I am glad at heart. Be ye also merry to-night, and to-morrow wiser.'

"And thus saying, the King gave them a purse of gold and turned away."

"What a little story," cried the young spiders.

"Hush!" answered Mrs. Grabem. "Now I must mend this hole in our cobweb. But, bless me! run to the den. Here comes a big fly."

Quick as could be they all ran into the dark passage and Mrs. Grabem stayed at the door. Pretty soon the fly flew near. He was a handsome gay fellow all over gold and purple and sparkling in the sun-light. He thought he would have a little of the nice gum which flowed from the apple tree bark, so he flew nearer, but just as he alighted his legs caught in the net and then what a fuss he made!

Buz, Buz, and pulled and bit, but it was in vain, for he was held fast by a long cobweb which allowed him to go a little way but no further.

Then Mrs. Grabem ran out, and pulled at the web, and drew him near, when all the little spiders began to sing, "We shall have a good breakfast."

"What! do you mean to eat me?" said Fuz-buz, the Fly. "I never hurt you."

"Oh no," said Mrs. Grabem, "you will do us a great deal of good very soon. You are a queer-looking fly any how. I hope you won't disagree with my children. Where do you live?"

"In Spain," replied Fuz-buz proudly. "I am a Spanish fly."

"Dear me," cried one of the spiders, "perhaps you can tell us some stories."

"I know a thousand fairy tales," said Fuz-buz.

"Oh mamma!" said one fat little spider, "It would be a shame to eat a thousand stories all at once. Let us keep him until he tells us nine hundred and ninety-nine tales, and then we can eat him afterwards."

"That I call good advice," cried Mrs. Grabem, and at once she fastened the cobweb so that poor Fuz-buz could walk just a little way from the web and no farther.

"And now," said she, "twice a day you must tell my children a story. But never let me find you trying to get away or I will eat you in a moment."

The young spiders could hardly wait.

"Quick!" they cried, "a story!" "a story!"

"What about?" replied Fuz-buz, glad to be spared.

"Oh about men, big men like Robert Bruce," said they, "and about a Princess too."

"Very well," returned Fuz-buz, "Don't eat me, and I will tell you no end of stories and the first shall be about

Lady Golden Hair and her Two Lovers, Prince Clever and Prince Sturdy.

"A long while ago, and far far away, a lady lived who had such beautiful locks that the people named her Lady Golden Hair. Folks said that when she was little, her fairy Godmother had so well woven three strands of sunshine with her curly tresses that it never got loose again, and I suppose this must have been so, because when at night she walked in the garden all the flowers woke up and looked about thinking the daylight had come.

"All day long her maidens combed her hair with combs of gold, and at evening sang to her of the beautiful Prince who would one day come across the seas and win her love for evermore.

"Many came and looked into her deep brown eyes, but none suited her, and so she shook her golden hair, and they went their ways again.

A *

"At length her Father the King said she must make up her mind to marry somebody.

"The Princess said, 'I will marry no one who does not own a Roc's egg, and no one who has not kissed me, and no one who has not a lock of hair to show exactly like my own. And no one shall kiss me, and no one ever shall have a lock of my hair, and where on earth will any one get a Roc's egg? and so how shall I ever be married? No, I never will marry anybody.'

"At this her Father was in despair, but as he thought that perhaps some one might be bright enough to outwit the Princess, he caused it to be proclaimed everywhere that the Lady Golden Hair would marry the man who had kissed her, and who could show a lock of hair just like hers, and who owned a Roc's egg.

"When her lovers heard this they all cried and went away, except two who were named Prince Clever and Prince Sturdy.

"Prince Clever was handsome and tall, and very cunning, because he was a Sorcerer's son, but Prince Sturdy was brave and straightforward, and had honest eyes of his own which were brown as garnets and as steady as stars.

"Now when these two heard about the Princess, and what must be done to marry her, Prince Clever said, 'I am so cunning that I shall be sure to succeed;' but

Prince Sturdy said, 'Thorns are roses to those who love! I will try.'

"When the Princess saw them she wished silently that Prince Sturdy might succeed; still she only said, 'How foolish you both must be. Do either of you own a Roc's egg?' and then she bade them good-bye and they kissed their hands to her and rode away by different paths till each of them entered a wood where they dismounted, and thought how to get a Roc's egg. 'Then,' said Clever, 'I see;' but Sturdy said, 'I will ride till I find one.'

"About a thousand miles away, across a great sea, lived a Roc who had just laid an egg as big as a house and as hard as marble. No one knew where she lived except a witch, to whose cave in a great hill Prince Clever rode swiftly.

"Because he was a Sorcerer's son the witch came out to speak to him. But, meanwhile, Prince Sturdy having become lost in the woods rode on, until at nightfall he heard voices.

"Then he alighted and clambered over the hill and lay quiet until he heard to his delight the witch telling Clever where to get the Roc's egg.

"As quick as could be Sturdy got on his horse and rode away as hard as ever a man could ride. By and by he came to the sea, where he hired a ship, and sailed many days to a desolate land where was nothing but hills of gray sand.

"Here he went on shore and sent the ship away. Then, drawing his sword, he climbed a great sand hill and after two days reached the top. There he saw in a mighty nest the great egg, as white and smooth as ivory.

"As soon as the Roc flew away to get her dinner the Prince came near and began to crack a big hole in the egg with his sword. Presently all the insides of the egg ran out of the hole and nearly drowned him. When it was well emptied and the whole of it had flowed away to the sea, the Prince put his bag of cakes into the egg, and then his sword, and at last squeezed himself in.

"He was just able to thrust his turban, into the hole, when the Roc flew home to her nest.

"When she left her nest once more Sturdy made a nice little opening as big as a pea, so that he could just see through it. And what think you he saw?

"There were two ships on the sea, and Prince Clever with a hundred men. Very soon they came up the hill and began to push the egg and to heave it over with crow-bars and beams of wood, until it rolled to the edge of the sand heap. Then to Prince Sturdy's horror the egg began to turn over and over down the hill to the sea.

"Fast it went, and faster and faster, while Sturdy tumbled over and over, and was on his head one minute,

and on his heels the next, till at last splash went the egg into the water and floated lightly on the rolling waves.

"Very soon the sailors tied a rope around the egg, and fastened the other end to their ships, and sailed away rejoicing.

"In this manner they sailed many weeks, until poor Sturdy had eaten his last cake and was nearly starved to death.

"When at last they came to land, the egg was hoisted on to a huge car, and a hundred horses drew it to the Palace of the Princess Golden Hair, while Prince Clever rode alongside as happy as could be.

"When the lady saw Clever and the egg she was ready to cry with vexation, because she knew there was only one Roc's egg in the world, and because Prince Clever had gotten it.

"Soon her father called her to welcome the Prince, and every one went to see the egg, while the music sounded and the people hurrahed for Prince Clever.

"As soon as he saw the lady he ran and knelt and said, 'Princess, here is my Roc's egg.'

"Then a voice was heard saying, 'No, it is mine!'

"'Who spoke?' said Clever.

"'I,' said the voice, 'It is mine!'

"But no one could tell where the voice came from.

"At last the Chief Magician cried aloud, 'Who dares to mock the King?'

2

"Then said the voice, 'Oh great Magician, who owns the house, he who lives in it, or he who looks at it?'

"'He who lives in it,' answered the Magician.

"'Then it is my egg,' said Sturdy, as he broke away the shell and stepped out of the hole in the side of the egg.

"'Ah,' said the lady to herself, 'what beautiful eyes he has.' But Prince Clever smote his breast, and the people hurrahed for Prince Sturdy.

"Meanwhile Sturdy knelt to the Lady. 'Ah,' said he, 'it is easy to live in a Roc's egg, or to storm a city for a Lady's love, but to kiss her and to find hair like thine, woe is me! How can these things be done?'

"As for Clever, he smiled, and said to himself, 'It is hard to bring a Roc's egg home, but to cheat a woman with a lock of hair and to steal a kiss is easy.'

"After Prince Clever had eaten and rested the two Princes kissed their hands to the lady and rode away once more to find a tress of hair which should be like that of the Princess.

"Now what did Prince Clever do to get the lady? He went into the country to see his fairy godmother and to ask her advice, and this was what she told him to do.

"He was to dress himself like a pedlar and was to take with him a beautiful great opal, and afterwards he was to do other things which presently you shall hear of.

"When the Fairy told him all these things he said,

'Ah Godmother, how shall I make my nose long and my mouth big and ugly so as to be like a real pedlar?'

" 'Well my dear,' she replied, 'that is easy,' and so saying she put a forefinger into the two corners of his mouth and pulled it until one corner was under each ear.

" 'I think that will do,' she said, 'and as to your nose, take a pinch of this snuff.'

" No sooner had he done as she desired than he began to sneeze so hard that in five minutes the end of his delicate nose was blown out into a great round purple knob, which was so bright that he could not keep from squinting to get a look at it.

" 'I do not think any one will know you now,' said the Fairy, 'but be careful not to open your mouth very wide or possibly your head may fall off backwards.'

" 'Upon my word,' cried the Prince when he looked at his face in a smooth pool of water, 'If I be as cunning as I am ugly I shall surely win the Lady !'

" The Fairy then gave him a little red cloak, and bade him walk like an old man and be careful.

" Finally she placed in his basket a gold box containing the magical opal.

" When he had left her she drew a ring on the ground and stood within it, and enchanted the Lady Golden Hair with wicked words, so that for four days and nights she had no sleep, because the instant her lids closed she dreamed that nine beautiful ladies were kissing Prince Sturdy, and that he was also kissing one of them and the one he kissed was not herself.

" So it was that all these days she lay awake angry, and all the while Prince Clever rode fiercely to her garden gate.

" Near by he hid his horse, and walking like an old man came to the Palace slowly and asked to see the Lady.

" The guard laughed at his nose and told him the Princess was ill and could not sleep.

" 'It is well,' answered he, 'I have a charm here to bring her sleep.'

"As soon as this was known he was quickly ordered to the chamber of the Princess, where resting on a couch she lay, while her ladies fanned her with fans made of fresh flowers which every ten minutes were brought to them by slaves.

"Although she felt very badly from want of sleep no sooner did she see the Prince with his new face than she began to laugh until she cried with mirth. 'For tears,' said Saadi the poet, 'are the diamonds of affliction and the pearls of merriment.'

"After a time however the Princess grew silent, although she did not dare to look at him when he talked. Now this was what he said,—'Here is an amulet for them that sleep not, or sleeping have evil dreams. Let thy ladies leave thee, and in a moment thou shalt sleep.'

" 'Instantly begone !' cried the Princess to her maidens. 'Fly ! I have no fears. Let a slave with a drawn scimetar keep the door and leave me with this wise and astonishing man.'

" Then, when there were none in the room but the Lady and himself, the Prince opened his gold box and lifted out of it a large opal which shone with a dim gray sleepy lustre with points of red and purple light.

"When he held the jewel up before her eyes she said, 'It has letters on it. What be they? What do they mean?'

2 *

" 'The words,' he replied, 'are the names of the nine most stupid books that ever were written, and within is the name of the sleepiest man that ever lived, and also the name of a very young baby who slept every night all night long.'

" 'It is well,' said the Princess. 'Let me sleep.'

" 'Rise !' said the Prince, and she stood erect while he held the opal before her eyes, and the golden flow of her hair fell from head to neck and from waist to floor in curves of darkling gold like the early sunlight when it is yet touched with the fading brown of twilight.

" As she gazed fixedly at the jewel her eyelids closed, and drowsy languor grew upon her face, till at last she swayed backwards and fell upon the couch.

" Then the Prince laid the jewel on the floor and crushed it with his foot. As it brake, a rosy flame flashed from it, and a heavy odorous smoke curled upwards and filled the room with dense vapour.

" Then the Prince took a long lock of her golden hair, and with his dagger cut it quickly. When he had twisted it around his sword hilt he leaned over and kissed her cheek, but though the Lady slept the blood seemed to leap to the spot he had touched, and her cheek grew scarlet, as he turned away ashamed and fled from the palace.

" Near to the garden he mounted his horse, and spurred swiftly away through the night, while the trees moaned

in the wind as he passed, and the birds awoke and sang,
'Shame! shame!' till he stopped his ears and fled faster
and faster.

"Thus it was that Prince Clever kissed the Lady and
had a golden lock to show which was like her own, because it was her own. The next day he met Sturdy.

"'Ha! ha!' said Clever, 'you own a Roc's egg, but I
have kissed the Lady, and who do you think has hair
like this?'

"'Only one,' replied Prince Sturdy sadly.

"'We shall· meet to-morrow,' said Clever, for so they
had agreed, and thus saying he rode away.

"Prince Sturdy also arose and entered a. wood near
by, for he was sick at heart and desired to see no man's
face.

"In a little while he was aware of two wild roses beside a rock on which he had seated himself. As he
thought of the Lady he wept, and just one tear fell upon
a rose.

"Then said a faint clear voice, 'The dew falls.'

"'I hope it is rain,' said another voice which was still
more sweet and pure.

"'Ah,' sighed the Prince, 'happy roses!'

"'Why do you weep?' said the roses, for it was their
voices he had heard.

"'Because I may not steal a lady's kiss,' said the

Prince, 'and because I want a tress of golden hair the like of which is not to be had on earth.'

"'We don't know much about kisses,' said the rose. 'But it is pleasant to touch a young rose bud when the winds blow us against one another. I suppose that is a kiss.'

"'Yes,' said Sturdy laughing, as he pushed the two roses together till their red lips touched.

"'Thanks,' said they. Then after a silence one of them said, 'If I were you I would go and lie on the top of a great cliff, and as the yellow sunlight trickles over the stones at morning, I would catch a bit in a gold box and shut the lid quickly and keep it. Where is a Lady would have golden locks like that, so yellow and so fine?'

"'It is well,' cried the Prince, and so saying he went away, sadly thinking of the kiss he might not have.

"Next day the Court and the King and the Princess were in the garden awaiting the two Princes.

"First came Prince Clever who had gotten his good looks again, and who came gaily with a hundred knights and with slaves who bore an ivory box which held the Princess' hair.

"Next came Prince Sturdy on a great black steed, but all alone and with only a little gold box in his hand.

"When both had bent before the lady she smiled and said, 'You are empty handed.'

"'No,' said Clever, and bade the slaves approach. Then from the ivory box he took a glorious tress of the Lady's hair.

"'Is it like?' said he. 'Ah!' she cried, as she matched it with her own long hair. 'It is the same! it was mine! How came you by this?'

"'Pardon me, Lady,' he said. 'It was I who in your sleep yesterday stole this tress of hair. Where else is any like it?'

"'Ah!' she cried, growing pale, 'You were the Sorcerer with the foul visage. You must have worn your heart upon your face for once Fair Sir. But ah me!' she continued, 'the kiss! the kiss! Did you dare to kiss me, sir Prince?'

"'I dared,' he said. 'How else could I win you?'

"'Enough,' she said, and turned, pale and despairing, to Prince Sturdy.

"'Lady,' said he, 'at morning I climbed the hill and caught in this box a tress of golden sunlight. If it be not as like to thy hair as sun to sun I am a false knight.' Then he opened the box beside the Lady's wealth of hair.

"'Bosh!' cried Prince Clever. 'There is nothing there,' for the box of a truth was empty.

"'True,' said Sturdy, 'It was bright this morning, but it is darkness now beside the sunshine of my Lady's locks.'

" 'Well said !' cried the King, while the Princess blushed like a whole summer of rosy peaches.

" 'By my beard !' cried Clever, 'He has the egg, and it seems I am outwitted about the lock of hair. I pray you to tell me which of us has the kiss.'

" 'A gift is better than a theft,' said she, and whispering this, bent down and kissed the brow of brave Prince Sturdy who trembled like a lily of earth in the wind of Paradise.

" But as for Prince Clever, he made a wry face and said, ' It is very warm in this place,' and so went away with his hands in his pockets and was no more seen among men."

When Fuz-buz had ended, all the little family of spiders began to rejoice together, because of the nice story they had heard and also because of the many more which were yet to be told.

The next afternoon as soon as ever Mrs. Grabem began to knit, the spiders cried aloud for a story.

" But I am tired," said Fuz-buz.

" No matter !" cried the spiders, "we are not."

" Come, no nonsense !" roared Mrs. Grabem.

" Well," cried poor Fuz-buz. " Let me think a little."

" I should not suppose it took much thinking to make up stories," replied Mrs. Grabem.

By this time Fuz-buz was ready and having eaten a little cherry gum to clear his throat, he began as follows :

" This is a fairy tale about

Cold Country.

About Trowel Ku the Beaver who builds Dams. About Kanecri the Loon who sings on the Lakes. About Hoota the Owl who is not so wise as he looks. About Weeska the Fox who is just as sharp as his own nose, and that is saying a great deal.

"Ever so many days ago," said Fuz-buz, "and ever so far away up among the great lakes it was always summer. There the trees were always green and the flowers never ceased to bloom nor the birds to sing.

"The beaver built dams and no winter came to freeze them. The owl hooted solemnly and the squirrels raced and played and ate nuts all the year, and the foxes joked with the big bears, and the loons sang to the stars all the nights long, and the stars winked at the lakes, and no one ate any one else, for every one was merry and happy, because it was summer all the year.

"But at last everything and everybody grew tired of being so happy.

"'Ah me!' said the bear, 'I get so fat it would be as easy to roll as to walk.'

"'Just so,' sighed the trees, 'what a bore to have to make leaves all the time.'

"Only the owl said, 'I'm comfortable,' and gave his feathers a lazy shake and went to sleep again.

" After a while all the animals and trees and fish had a great talk and made up their minds that it was unpleasant to have hot weather always.

" So the fox proposed that they should go in search of cool weather, and bring back a little by way of a change.

" At last they agreed to send Trowel Ku the Beaver, and Kanecri the Loon, and Hoota the Owl, and Weeska the Fox.

" All were ready except Hoota the Owl, who said, ' I'm comfortable. What's the use?' and fell asleep again, but Weeska bit his toes and Kanecri the Loon sang in his ears and at last they woke him up. 'For,' said the Beaver, ' he looks so wise we cannot do without him.'

" Therefore it was resolved that Trowel Ku the Beaver should pull out one of his feathers every five minutes to keep him wide awake, and having thus planned the matter each one filled a birch bark bag with food, and the whole party set off at daybreak.

" After a long journey they came to the hut of a magician called a Manitou, on a high hill. Here the Loon called aloud, but no one came until the Owl mounted on the Fox's back and knocked at the door, when a little hunch-backed woman opened it and said, ' You can't come in without money.'

" ' Ha ! ha !' said the Fox and ran away into the wood, and presently came back with a handful of green leaves which he gave to the old woman.

" ' That will do,' said she, for she was blind. 'Money must be plenty where you live. Come in.' By and by the Manitou came home.

" ' What now ?' said he.

" ' Sir,' answered Trowel Ku, the Beaver, 'I am tired of summer and of building dams. Tell us where we can buy a little cold to take home for a change.' 'And I,' said the Fox, 'I find it always too hot.' 'For my part,' cried the Loon, Kanecri, 'You have given us only summer. Either give me fewer feathers or else a little cold. As for the trees they are all growling about having no rest at making leaves.'

" ' Then,' said Manitou to the Owl, 'What do you want?' 'I'm comfortable,' said Hoota the Owl, and straightway went to sleep.

" ' Well,' said Manitou, 'I will send you to the cold country and you can all of you take home a bag of cold to your friends.' Then he began to laugh, and taking a deer-skin bade them all jump inside.

" When they were all in he sewed them up and putting the skin outside of the hut bade it go.

" At once it became alive and bounded off over the hills and through the streams until it came to a great frozen lake.

" Here the Beaver heard a noise, and presently an arrow went through the deer which fell on the ice. The

next moment a knife ripped the deer open, and the Owl
and the Beaver and Fox and Loon jumped out.

"Then they saw two tall men made of icicles who gave
a cry when they saw them, dropped their knives, and
skated away over the lake.

"'Dear me!' said Trowel Ku, 'This must be cold
land, let us fill our bags,' cried Weeska the Fox, 'and be
off.' 'Here is too much cold for me, I'm not comfortable,'
said Hoota the owl. 'Boo hoo how it bites my toes!'

"Then they all filled their birch bags with cold, of
which there was plenty for every one lying about loose,
and set off homewards.

"But after a little while they all became so cold that
their jaws chattered. By and by they saw the Manitou.

"'What now?' said he.

"'Too much cold,' said the Beaver. 'I think one bag
would answer,' added the Fox, 'and we could carry it by
turns.' 'I'm not comfortable,' groaned Hoota the Owl,
'my toes are frozen.' 'Suppose,' said the Loon, 'you
were to help us to carry the cold home.'

"'Ho!' answered Manitou, for he was very angry.
'Begone! you wanted summer and I gave it to you, and
you had leave to take as much cold as you wanted, and
were greedy and took too much. I will warm you a
little and send your cold home too.'

"Thus saying he tore the sunset out of the west and
threw it a thousand miles into their country, and lo! it fell

on the trees, and some it stained yellow and some red and some brown, which so amazed them that they let their leaves fall in affright and horror.

"Next the Manitou took up the bags of cold and threw them after the sunset, and as they flew they broke, and the white cold fell in little fleecy blankets on the naked trees and on the land.

"When the animals reached home there was no summer. So the Fox Weeska ran into his den in the rocks, and the Beaver Trowel Ku cried, 'Woe is me! the water has become white stone,' and the Loon Kanecri sang a song to the stars and flew up into the skies and sailed away and away. But Hoota the Owl said, 'I'm comfortable,' and fell fast asleep in a hollow stump."

The next night Mrs. Grabem herself came along with her little ones to hear Fuz-buz relate a tale.

"Be sure it is a nice story," said one of the spiders.

"For my part," cried Mrs. Grabem, "I take no interest in stories, but it pleases me to see the youngsters amused. You may go on while I knit, and as I have ten threads to mend let the story be a long one."

"Please ma'am," answered Fuz-buz, "I will now tell you a story which I flatter myself is the very best one I ever heard. It was brought by a cousin of mine from Bagdad where he got it from a very aristocratic fly who lived many years in the household of Sinbad the Sailor."

The Fountain of Youth.

"Once upon a time there lived in Persia a great king.
He had one nephew who was to be the ruler after him,
and to have all his kingdom.

"When this lad was about six years old a daughter
was born to the King. No sooner was her birth known
than the magicians foretold that she would be beautiful,
and would have blue eyes like lakes, which last was not
very hard to foretell because they were already blue, but
the magi also declared that on the day of her marriage
the King would die.

"'Oh ho!' said the King, who was called Omar, 'If
this be so she shall never marry, and I shall live long and
pleasantly, and after me she shall be queen. As for my
nephew, I fear that he may wish to be king when he
grows to manhood. Therefore let him be thrown into
the sea.' Then an old Magician arose and spoke thus.

"'Be careful, oh King, not to do this wicked act, or if
you greatly dread the Prince Ali give him to me, and I
will carry him far away to an island on the coast, where
he may be taught as a Prince should be, and where he may
live all his days and never know what he might have
been.'

"Then said a second counsellor, 'For my part I
advise that the Princess be shut up in a palace around
whose gardens a wall shall be built, that she may grow

up and see none but women, for so only can you make sure that she will not fall in love and marry.'

"'It were well,' said the King. 'Let the Magician take the Prince as he has said.' Accordingly the next day Prince Ali was carried to an island many miles from the main land and lodged in a fair palace. Here he was cared for by trusty persons who taught him all manner of wisdom, as well as to ride and hunt and swim, so that he grew up brave and handsome and full of goodness and knowledge.

"Meanwhile the Princess lived alone with her women in a gleaming marble castle which looked across the sea, and was girt about by a high wall on every side but that bounded by the waters of the ocean.

"The busy years went on and by and by the little girl grew to be a stately woman, and the Prince a tall and vigourous man, while the King Omar became gray and old, and was every day more greedy to live. Each morning he sent a slave to see how the Princess fared, and every month he was told all about Prince Ali, and so made sure of his constant safe keeping.

"One fine morning just after a storm a strange thing happened to the Prince. He was walking up and down the beach and looking at the waves which were rushing up the shore and sweeping down again with a fierce roar, when he heard a cry of distress among the rocks near by. In a moment he climbed towards the spot and

3 *

saw to his great wonder as he came near long tresses of
something like thin seaweed floating in the wind from a
rock above him. He seized it and was more amazed to find
that it was beautiful hair like his own, but of a bright
green colour. As he pulled it he heard again a cry of
pain which hastened his steps.

"This hair was wonderful, for it not only fell far down
the cliff but lay on top of the rocks and across bushes,
and was strung here and there with coral and great
pearls.

"When the nimble Prince had traced it some thirty
feet it led him to a deep hollow between two rocks. Into
this he descended. As he reached the bottom what
should he see but a little old woman, with fins for hands
and a long scaly tail like that of a fish. She was such a
comical little old lady that the Prince sat down and
laughed for five minutes. He ceased his mirth, however,
when the old creature waved her fins in a helpless way
and groaned aloud.

"'What can I do for you Mrs. Woman-fish?' said he,
'and how came you here?'

"'My dear,' said she, 'I am, as you see, a mermaid. I
happened to come on shore last night just to do a little
knitting by the light of the moon, when up came a big
storm, and the waves gave me a great toss over these
rocks and into this hole. But the worst of it is I have
lost my spectacles, and my poor back is nearly broken,

and one fin's out of joint, and I've lost a knitting-needle
and my back comb. Now if you would kindly carry me
to the edge of the rocks and throw me in, I think I could
reach home, but, as you may notice, I don't get along
very well upon land.'

"The Prince was too good-natured to refuse, so he
lifted her carefully, and drawing her long hair after him
climbed with his queer load to the top of the cliff. Here
he gave her a mighty cast, and away she went fifty feet
down into the sea with her green hair sailing after her.
The moment she felt the water she rolled over and
kissing her fin to Prince Ali sculled away as cleverly as
could be.

"The Prince said nothing about this adventure, but
felt sorry that he had not asked her some questions, for
you must know that whenever he asked questions of the
people who waited on him, and taught him, they were
very apt to say, 'Oh don't bother me! I'm busy,' so that
there were many things which he desired to learn and
could not.

"From this day forward he spent all of his time upon
the shore and among the rocks. At last one evening he
saw a large white crested wave rolling in, and on a sudden out of it paddled the mermaid. She sculled up the
sand and rolling over on her back said to the Prince, 'My
dear I can never thank you enough. If the doctors had

been quicker about getting my flapper well I should have
been here long ago.'

"'You are most welcome,' returned Ali, 'and the more
so because perhaps you can tell me who I am.'

"'Sir!' said she, 'You are a King's son. Your
parents are dead, and your uncle has put you here for
fear that you may wish to take the kingdom away from
his daughter the Princess Jessalie who is the most beautiful woman in the world. She also is a prisoner within
the gardens of her Palace because it has been foretold
that whenever she marries, her Father the King will die.'

"'Would that I could see her!' said the Prince.

"'Sir!' replied the mermaid, 'to-morrow I will bring
you her picture, and meanwhile here are some trifles
which my children have sent you as tokens of their
gratitude.'

"Thus saying she shook her head and a double handful
of pearls fell from her hair and dropped at the feet of the
Prince, after which the mermaid tumbled into the water
and swam deftly away.

"The next morning early Ali went to the beach and
found the mermaid waiting with a large piece of crystal
in her flappers.

"'Prince,' she said, 'Yesterday the Princess Jessalie
chanced to look into a small pool of water on the shore
where she walks. As quick as could be I enchanted the
pool and turned it into a crystal mirror, so that the face

of the Princess is fixed upon it forever. Look, I have brought it away with me.'

"At once the Prince regarded the mirror, and this was what he saw in it. Calm lazy eyes of blue, and below them cheeks dimpled and rosy, and twin lips which made you jealous of each, because ever they kissed one the other, and brown hair which must have fallen down about this face as it looked into the pool of water, and blue around it all, the heavens which spread above her as she had bent to gaze at her own fairness.

"'Ah!' said Ali, 'This is my fate! Take me to this woman swiftly that I may see her and die contented.'

"'Not so,' said the mermaid, 'be guided by me and in time you shall marry her. Give me a message and I will carry it to the Princess, but as yet she must not know your name, or it might be that the King hearing it would put you to death. Speak your message to this shell and I will answer for the rest.'

"Thus saying she pointed to a white shell which lay on the beach. The Prince took it up, and laughing, whispered a few words in its curled lip, and then as the mermaid bade him threw it far out into the sea.

"'Now,' said the mermaid, 'If you tell a lady once that you love her she laughs. If you tell her twice she is angry, but when you have ten times said 'I love,' she will either hate or love you, or perhaps may hate and love by turns, each for five minutes as sometimes doth

chance. Now, therefore, many times you must say to
her I love you.'

"But *how* shall I do this?' asked Prince Ali.

" 'Sir,' she said, 'look upwards and clap your hands
thrice.'

"Without further words the young man did as he was
told, when instantly a great white swan descended from
a vast height and alighted on the water's edge beside
them. The mermaid at once began to dig in the sand,
and presently found a large oyster shell which she desired
Ali to open. As he did so a necklace of pearls fell out,
the like of which no jeweller ever saw before or since.

" 'Now!' said the mermaid, 'hang this on the swan's
neck for a present to the Princess, and with thy finger
write on the bird's breast a message.'

"The Prince was lost in wonder, but without hesita-
tion he traced a few rapid letters on the white breast of
the swan. As he wrote, the feathers where he touched
them grew scarlet, so that you might read in red letters
'I love thee,' marked on the snowy whiteness of the
swan's bosom.

"Scarcely had he made an end of this short letter of
love when the swan rose in swift flight until she was no
longer to be seen by the amazed Prince, who turned to
look at the mermaid, though only to find that she too had
vanished. Then in still greater wonder Ali walked
homeward along the water's edge.

"Thus many days went by and brought no change, for ever the west winds blew, and ever the waves climbed the shore and laid soft cheeks on the sands and whispered, and went backward moaning again.

"This sadness pleased the Prince who lay on the rocks all day and heard the sobbing waters, and looked wearily over the wide green ocean fields where the bubble-crested foam came and went from sight like the white clover blossoms which swayed amid their fields of green, when the wind leaped across the rocks and took its pleasure inland.

"One of these days the Princess walked on the shore with her women, when the youngest of them said, 'What a lovely shell!' 'Let me hear what it says,' cried the Princess; but no sooner had she put it to her ear than the shell murmured softly, 'I LOVE YOU.'

"'Ah!' said the Princess Jessalie to the oldest of her ladies, 'This shell sings to me words new and strange. Tell me I pray you what is LOVE?'

"She had scarcely finished when all the old ladies held up their hands in horror, for this and all other such words were forbidden within the Palace bounds. The more they made faces and signs at her the more the Princess wished to know. So she kept saying continually, 'What is love? I will know what is love.'

"But no one answered, and some of the old ladies cried, and some ran away, for they all feared that King

Omar would strangle them because the Princess had heard the forbidden word, and because no one of them knew but that presently she would say, 'what is a man?' or some other such dreadful words.

"When at length the Princess found herself alone with her governess, she said again, 'What is love?'

"'My dear child,' replied the old lady, 'it is a kind of medicine!'

"'Ah!' cried the Princess, 'Then I see why the ladies made faces when I spoke of it. I suppose they had all taken a dose. But it sounds very pleasant,' she added, and all day long she went about with the shell at her ear.

"The next morning the shell was gone, for the ladies had taken it away so that they might prevent further mischief by hiding this wonderful shell. But before they concealed it they listened to hear it say 'I love you.' No one listened twice, and they all said the shell was an ill-bred shell and had no manners, though what it said to them I know not, perhaps something true but not pleasant.

"The next day while walking in the garden the Princess asked eagerly about her singing shell. While everybody pretended to look for it a whirring noise was heard and a fluttering of white wings was seen as the swan lit at the feet of the lady and shook the pearl necklace into her lap.

"'Oh marvellous!' cried the Princess, 'come quickly look at this! see what pearls! and Mahomet preserve us! Bismillah! Here is the name of that medicine again, written in scarlet on the breast of this beautiful swan, 'I LOVE THEE.'

"No sooner had the old ladies seen these fatal words than they rushed at the bird and beat it so cruelly that it had hard work to get away even with the help of the Princess herself.

"This time she was so urgent to be told more, and so eager in her questions, that the matter came to the quick ears of the King Omar her father. At once the guards around her Palace gardens were doubled. Twelve old ladies were set to work to gather up all the shells along shore, while twelve more were ordered to keep strict watch lest any other messages of love should come to the fair Jessalie.

"Meantime none knew whence came these strange words, and the King grew more and more angry and alarmed whenever he thought about it.

"All his precautions were in vain. One fine morning every rose-leaf in the gardens had written upon it in golden Arabic letters, 'I LOVE YOU.'

"This drove the King wild, and he commanded all the rose-bushes in the kingdom to be cut down, which was instantly done.

"The next morrow at day-break a great noise was

heard, and when the Princess arose and peeped from her window every bird in the garden was singing, 'I LOVE YOU, I LOVE YOU, I LOVE YOU.'

"This time the King ordered the Princess to be shut up in the Palace.   Then the birds were driven away and a great silken net hung over the garden so that the voice of the birds might no more be heard singing this sweet treason among the flowers.

"Very soon, however, the Princess became so weary of her Palace that she fell ill, and no one dared to tell the King that all night long in dreams she whispered, 'I LOVE YOU, I LOVE YOU.'

"Far and near the King sought counsel of all manner of wise men and doctors, but no one would venture to order medicine for the Princess without seeing her, and as to a man doing that, it was out of the question.

"About this time the mermaid, who I need not say was the merrymaker of all this mischief, met the Prince on the beach one evening and thus addressed him.

"'The Princess whom you love is ill, because she has not found out who it is that is ever saying through the shells and the birds and the flowers, "I love you." Take therefore this mirror, write on it a letter with your finger tip, and I will see that it reaches the Princess.'

"The Prince gladly followed these directions, for though when he had traced words on the glass he could see nothing of them, he felt sure of the mermaid's power to help him.

"When he had ended she took the mirror, and carrying it all the way above the waves hastened to the mainland. When she came to the shore she put on a long petticoat to hide her scaly fish tail, and drawing her fins through the sleeves of a gown, mounted up on a pair of crutches and hobbled with great labour to the Palace of King Omar. Here she told the guard to let the King know that a lame doctoress who had come from a far country was waiting to cure the Princess.

"So soon as ever the King heard this he ordered her to be admitted. When he set eyes upon her odd figure he cried out,

"'Quick! old woman speak! and that shortly! If you can cure my daughter say so.'

"'Oh King!' she answered, 'Let the lady look into this mirror, but see that no one touches it on the way. Let the Princess breathe upon it as she looks, and if it does not cure her throw me into the sea without mercy.'

"'Well said!' cried the King. 'It shall be as you desire. Let the mirror be carried to the Princess.'

"Accordingly that evening the crystal was taken to the Palace with every care and given to Jessalie.

"'You have but to breathe on it,' said her Governess, 'and you will be well.'

"'Give it to me,' she said, and instantly blew a breath

upon its polished surface. As she did so, to her great amazement she read these words which seemed to come into view on the glass as her breathing moistened it, 'I LOVE YOU. I, THE PRINCE ALI YOUR COUSIN, I LOVE YOU.'

"As her breath faded from the glass the words fled from sight, but the Princess fell back murmuring, 'My cousin Ali, he loves me.'

"Then there was confusion. The ladies tore their hair and screamed aloud, and the slaves beat their breasts, while the Princess fainted away. In a moment the news came to the King that his daughter had no sooner seen the mirror than she had called aloud the name of her cousin and fainted.

"'Allah !' muttered the King, 'Well said the poet, "A daughter is an aching tooth, and he who doth not beat his child shall one day strike his knees in vain." Let this old hag of a doctor be cast into the sea,' he added, ' and let the captain of the guard take ship speedily and slay this nephew of mine whom I did ill to spare so long.'

"Accordingly the mermaid was taken to the rocks and thrown a hundred feet down into the waves, where she laughed a little, and kicking off her petticoats swam away merrily to see the Prince, for whose safety she had great fears.

"Just as she reached the island she saw the Prince

standing on a rock and bravely defending himself against the guard of the King.

"As quick as could be the mermaid called to him to leap off of the rocks into the sea, for although he had killed at least a dozen of his foes he was faint and sorely pressed. When he heard her call he smote the captain of the guard a fierce blow, and bounding up the rocks hesitated an instant, and then leaped boldly into the foaming waters at their feet.

"For a moment he felt his strength fail, then he saw a thousand colours before his eyes, then a gray mist came over them, and after that darkness, until he awakened as from a dream of death.

"When he became conscious, he was under the water seated at the foot of a vast tree of coral. About him was a forest of like trees, hung with huge pearls and covered with sea-weed of many tints, among which great fish and nameless ocean beasts floated lazily to and fro.

"'Come,' said the mermaid, 'You are now a son of the sea. Let us go.'

"Upon this he arose and in a great maze of wonder walked along, while the mermaid swam easily by his side. Sometimes they passed huge heaps of amber, and sometimes turned aside from the wrecks of mighty ships, or else trode through caverns whose sand was gold dust and gleaming jewels, till at length they came to a vast wall of rock.

4 *

"Here the mermaid knocked and a door opened and let them into a mighty hall builded throughout of the purest jasper.

"But what the Prince saw here no one will ever know, for here the mermen and mermaids lived, and here they made the Prince so welcome that he would never have wished for earth again if the Princess whom he loved had only been with him.

"Meanwhile King Omar felt himself growing old and feeble, but the nearer he came to death the more he desired to live. Then there came into his head a cunning way to cheat the Angel of Death. He therefore summoned his counsel and spake to them thus,

"'It has been foretold that I shall die when my daughter marries. Now let proclamation be made that whosoever shall bring to me a cup of water from the fountain of youth shall have the Princess for his wife. So shall I drink of the water and become young again, and that which was to kill me shall bring me life.'

"Then there was silence awhile till at last an aged Mufti arose.

"'Oh King!' said he, 'Beware how you resist the words of fate. Is it so easy to live rightly that you would crave for more of life? He who lengthens the life of this world makes shorter the life of the world to come. Beware!'

" 'Fool !' said the King, 'thou art ten years younger than I. Let it be as I have said.'

" Soon after this the mermaid said to Ali, 'It is time Prince that you left us. The King desires a cup of the fountain of youth, and to him who brings it he will give the Princess. Therefore have no fear, but take thy sword and this crystal flask, and passing through yonder gateway journey on until you reach a deep valley, at the bottom of which you will find the fountain. Drink none, but fill your flask and hasten to the King without pause or fear.'

" With this counsel the Prince took his sword, and tying the flask about his neck set out. As he stepped through the gate-way of amber he looked up and saw above him the splendid blue of the deep sea like one vast quiet sapphire. Before him a gradual slope led downwards over rocks and sea grasses which at last ceased, and he came upon a floor of sand whiter than the purest snow.

" As the descent ended he saw in front of him a majestic angel of vast height. Her foot rested on a marble skull of huge proportions, and upon her brow was written *Azrael.*

" For a moment the Prince paused in dread ; then he took courage and said humbly,

" 'Is this the fountain of youth ?' As he ceased the angel murmured, '*Out of death cometh all life,*' and solemnly struck the skull with her wand. Instantly a purple liquid gushed from under the skull and floated in slow spirals upward through the still water.

"With a bound the Prince knelt at the skull, filled his flask and turned away in haste, for already the purple color was tinting the whole sea about him, and he remembered well the mermaid's warning.

"Three days after this Ali reached the court of King Omar. To his great joy he found the court sitting, and the King on his throne.

"So splendid was Prince Ali's dress and so noble his air that no one stopped him, and he entered freely and unquestioned. Before him sat the King his uncle. He was very old, but still vigourous enough to live for many years beyond the common span of human life.

"Ali listened while the Muftis read aloud the promise of the King that whosoever brought the cup of water from the fountain of youth should marry the Princess Jessalie.

"No sooner had they ended than Ali bowed before the throne.

"'Oh King!' said he, 'I am the Prince Ali, thy nephew, whom you would have slain. I have brought to you here a cup of the water of the fountain of youth, Drink, but read first what words have come on the flask since I filled it at the fountain. Drink then if you will, and give me the Princess, for by my sword this is water of the fountain of youth and none other.'

" ' Ha !' said the King, ' Give it to me !' and tottering he arose and descending a few steps seized the flask. Then he tore from it the silver cover with which the Prince had sealed it.

" At once a dense purple vapour rose in clouds from the lip of the flask and curled upwards through the hall. Whosoever breathed of this his eyes flashed and he dreamed of mornings long ago, and of fair women and of boyhood, so that all who felt it stood bewildered.

" Then cried the King, ' I drink to youth !' and would have drained the flask, but Ali held his hand and bade him read the words which were graven upon the vessel.

" ' It is but a moment to wait for youth,' cried the King, and turning to a magician bade him read the words, ' For,' said he, ' I am old and my sight fails me.'

" ' Oh my master !' said the magician, ' These are the words :

> " ' He who steals to-morrows
> Shall drink the wine of sorrows.' "

" Then the aged counsellor fell back with an altered face as he breathed the purple fumes, ' Woe is me ! I am stronger ! I am grown younger ! Woe is me ! I am further from Allah.'

" But the King, saying no word, set the flask to his lips and drained it to the utmost drop. Then with a cry of delight he threw the vessel away, and shouting aloud, ' I

am young again!' bounded up the steps and pausing
faced the mutely wondering crowd.

"When he turned he was seen as a man in the lusty
vigour of life, stalwart and strong of limb.

"'Ho!' he said, 'my guard!' but none stirred, for his
face was still changing, and now his beard was gone, and
it was a lad who sat upon the throne, and a lad's voice
which cried aloud.

"'This man to the dungeons! What ho! my guard!'
And yet they moved not, for the lad was now a child.

"Still the stern will worked, and the child-King said
faintly, 'My guards! my guards!' till his voice broke into
baby lispings, and now it was an infant who sat upon
the throne.

"Then the changes seemed to cease, and the ancient
counsellor who had so wisely warned the King cried aloud,
'Allah il Allah! great and wonderful are thy ways!'

"When one man had thus broken silence a mighty
tumult arose, amidst which the baby King looked right
and left with blue eyes of wonder.

"But Ali drew his sword and in a terrible voice
ordered the guard to clear the hall. Instantly he was
obeyed, and then there was great counsel held as to what
should be done with the King. At length it was decided
that he should be sent to the island where Ali had lived,
and be kept there all his days. These indeed proved few,
for it is recorded in the chronicles of the kingdom that he

took teething rather hard, and died in his second summer of malignant whooping-cough.

"As to Prince Ali he married his cousin the Princess Jessalie, and the mermen and the mermaids came to the wedding and brought with them for presents pearls and amber and tortoise shells such as folks never see now-a-days.

"They lived long together, and loved one another well, and they both died at one and the same moment, which was the happiest thing of all their happy lives."

The sun was not yet down on the next evening when the young spiders began to collect around Fuz-buz.

"Tell us," said one of them, "a story about giants."

"There's a jolly idea," cried another. "Is it to be a spider giant?"

"Ahem!" replied Fuz-buz. "I wish there were such giants, and I wish one of them would come along this very moment and gobble you all up."

This he said in so fierce a voice that the young spiders ran away squealing so loud that if you had been a spider and had owned an ear-trumpet, you might have heard them at least three inches off.

As for Mrs. Grabem she hurried in a rage to Fuz-Buz, and gave him a shake, saying, "Have a care old rascal, how you scare my young ones. Tell them a story at once, or you shall never tell another on this earth."

"Yes, madam," answered Fuz-buz very meekly, and as soon as ever he could get his breath he began as follows, to tell them the story of Krusstikuss and Growlegrum.

Krusstikuss and Growlegrum.

"There have been many giants I believe, but there never were any others like the great giant Growlegrum and his twin brother Krusstikuss.

"These two giants were both of them Ogres. Their mother was an Afrite, and their grandfather a Ghoul. On which account they were probably the most unpleasant giants that anybody ever came across.

"When very young they were tall and stout, but one day unluckily for Krusstikuss, his grandmother, who was a fat giantess, sat down on him.

"Not feeling anything in particular she fell asleep and did not awaken for three months.

"Of course it was hard for Krusstikuss to grow while his grandmother sat upon him, so he began to spread out sideways and never afterwards got out of the habit. He therefore became as fat as a bun, while his brother Growlegrum grew as tall as the highest tree.

"So one was tall, and one stout, but both were of the same size in wickedness, and as to Krusstikuss he liked to eat babies, while Growlegrum was fond of young ladies, although their hoops sometimes disagreed with him.

"When these monsters grew up they ate so many people that their father told them they would cause a famine, and must go away and find another land where people were more plenty.

"At last they took his advice and started out together to seek a new home. After eating a great many folks they came to a beautiful country where lived a King who had a daughter as good as she was pretty.

"When the two giants reached the borders of this land they sat down and began to talk.

"'I am getting so big,' said Krusstikuss, 'that I find it a labour to walk about and look for babies. They must be very scarce.'

"'Not more so than young ladies,' cried Growlegrum. 'I should think they would like to be eaten before they grow to be old and ugly, but really it does not seem so.'

"While they were thus lamenting the scarcity of food, an old woman with a red cap and a green kirtle came from the wood and stood before them.

"'Sirs,' said she, 'I am a cousin of yours, and also a witch. Why should you be troubled about your meals? Order the King Hassan to send hither twice every day ten fat babies and one young lady.'

"'Good,' said the giants, 'we can lie on these hills and eat and sleep without labour. So let it be. Go you to King Hassan and tell him to send us the babies and the

5   C

young ladies without fail, or else we will eat him and fry him first.'

" This made the old witch chuckle, and she went away quickly towards the city with her wicked news. Presently she entered the Palace, for she was a cousin of the King, and went straight to the garden where she told King Hassan that the two giants were on the borders of his country, and must have ten babies and a young lady twice a day or else they would eat the King and fry him first, which made Hassan feel hot all over.

. " He soon saw that he could do nothing against such vast monsters, and therefore beat his breast and ordered his captains to take to the giants the babies and the young ladies.

" You may be sure that when this happened twice a day for a week folks began to be very much troubled. By and by the mammas hid away the babies in tree-tops and chimnies and in all sorts of out of the way places. And as to young ladies there were none to be found, for every one of them put on her brother's pantaloons, and it was hard work to catch a woman at all.

" It chanced about this time that the Princess was walking in a wood near the Palace when she saw a young girl crying. Now as the Princess was very kind-hearted she stopped at once and said,

" ' Why do you cry ? What ails you ?'

" ' Oh dear !' said the other, ' to-morrow I am to be

taken by the guard to be eaten by the Ogres, Growlegrum
and Krusstikuss, and when I am gone who will comfort
my old mother, for she has no child but me?'

"When the Princess heard this she told her to wait a
little, and went herself to find the King.

"'Father,' said she, 'it is hard that all the young girls
should be eaten alive by these false giants. Why do not
you raise an army and go and fight and kill them? It is
base to give up to them in this way. Were I a man I
would slay them myself.'

"'It would be in vain to try,' answered the King.
'Well,' said the Princess, 'to-morrow I shall go alone in
place of the maiden who is chosen, and perhaps some good
knight will not willingly let me die so mean a death.'

"The King was very angry, but the Princess was
obstinate. Then a young Prince who was present arose
and said,

"'I have come, lady, a thousand miles to help you.
My name is Prince Bluets, and I am the great-grandson
of John, who is sometimes called Jack, the Giant Killer.
Go to the giants as you have said and all will yet be well.'

"Then the Princess looked and saw that the Prince
had brave eyes and was fair of face, so she replied,

"'It shall be as you say.'

"'To-morrow, then,' continued the Prince, 'you shall
go to the giants and I will follow you. But first take
this amulet and hang it around your neck. So long as

you wear it all things living and dead will love you, and no giant will wish to eat you.'

"Thus saying he hung around her neck a gold chain, and at once she went away and ordered her horse to ride to the giants. Meanwhile it was proclaimed that out of love for her people the Princess was going to beg the giants to go away and not to eat any more babies.

"As for the Princess, she sent word to the little maiden in the wood that she was going in her place, and then bravely mounted her horse and rode through the town to the gate.

"No sooner did the people see her than they began to follow her, because the amulet made every one wish to be near to her. But at the gate she bade them return, and rode away alone into the wood, though even there the charm still worked, and all things loved her more and more. The sun stared her in the eyes like a gallant over-bold, and the wind played with her chestnut hair and was happy, and the leaves bent down and kissed her, and all the mice and the birds and the bears and the foxes came out and followed her.

"But when she came near to the two Ogres and saw them sitting on a hill with their white eyes and rough faces and great black teeth like marble tombstones, all the animals set up a dismal howl and ran away. Yet still the lady rode along, and presently the two giants became aware of her presence.

"Then said Growlegrum, 'Here comes dinner,' but when she drew nearer he added, 'She's too pretty to eat. Who are you my dear?'

"'I am the Princess Violet,' said she, 'the King's daughter.'

"'Hah!' said both of the Ogres, 'You shall be my wife.'

"'Well,' cried she, 'I cannot have two husbands; put me in a safe place and after I have known you both for a month I can decide which I will have for my husband.'

"'Good,' returned Krusstikuss, 'So let it be.' Then they lifted her gently and put her near by in a castle whose owner they had devoured, and every day they brought her goodies to eat, enough for twenty dinners.

"In the morning came Growlegrum and looked over the castle wall and said, 'I love you my dear.' But in the afternoons came Krusstikuss and said, 'Bless me! how I love you!' Now the Princess knew that within a month she should hear of Prince Bluets.

"As for that Prince he went away to a magician and asked him how he could become thin.

"'There are four ways,' answered the magician,

> 'Eat nothing,
> 'Fall in love,
> 'Become jealous, and
> 'Think ever so much.'

"Then said the Prince, 'The advice is good,' and so

5 *

saying he gave him three links of a gold chain which he wore, and mounted his horse and rode swiftly until he came to a high hill which at a great distance overlooked the castle where the lady was. Here he sat down and with his spy-glass looked until he saw Krusstikuss kissing his great hand to the lady.

"This made him horribly jealous, and at once he began to get thin. Then for four days he ate nothing and so became thinner and thinner. Of course he was miserably in love, and this also made him lose flesh.

"After four days he was still too fat, so he began to think of all the hard conundrums and riddles and charades that ever were heard of, but at last when he had been two days thinking how to make apple pies out of donkies he became so thin that his bones were no thicker than walking sticks, and when he stood sideways he had no shadow at all.

"Then he took his sword and walking carefully for fear of breaking into halves or of being blown away, he descended the hill, and late at night knocked at a side door of the castle where the Princess Violet now lived.

"As soon as she heard the noise she came to the door and said,

"'Who is it?'

"'It is I,' answered the Prince, but his voice was so thin that he could hardly be heard, and if the Princess had not loved him she never would have been able to hear a word he said.

" 'My love,' he cried, 'It is I, Prince Bluets. Presently I shall squeeze my head through the key-hole, and you must then seize me by the hair and drag me in.'

"Of course giants' castles have very large key-holes, and as the Prince was as thin as could be he easily pushed his head through the key-hole, when the Princess took hold of his hair, and pretty soon drew him into the castle.

"She was very much amazed when she saw him so lean and meagre, but the Prince explained it all and they sat down and had a good talk until morning, when the Prince hid away in a corner under some hay.

"By and by came Krusstikuss, and looking over the castle wall said in a large voice, 'I love you my dear. Here are some nice little dishes for breakfast?' and so saying, he emptied his pockets of about two wagon loads of cakes and candy and bon-bons and all kind of goodies such as Princesses eat.

" 'Sir,' said the Princess, 'If I am to be a giant's wife, I must learn to eat babies. If you love me you will bring me all the babies you get, that I may keep them until they get so fat and tender that I shall be tempted to eat them.'

" 'But what shall I live on myself?' cried Krusstikuss.

" 'Oh !' said the Princess, 'if you are in love you will not care to eat.'

"'That's queer,' returned the giant, 'but I suppose it won't hurt me to suck my paws for awhile like the bears.'

"Then he took four babies out of his hat and two out of his pockets, saying, 'I am sorry, but I ate four on the way. To-morrow you shall have all, and when you get them fat enough I will come and dine with you.'

"After this he went away leaving the babies to the Princess, who put them all in a row and fed them with nine dough-nuts apiece, so that if they did not get fat it was not her fault.

"In the afternoon came Growlegrum, who was as big in length as Krusstikuss was sideways.

"'My love,' said he, when he had peeped over the wall, 'What's this? Babies.'

"'Sir,' she replied, 'Your brother loves me, and has promised me all the babies, that I may fatten them. If you also love me at all, you will give me the young ladies you were to eat every day, that I may have some one to take care of the babies and feed them.'

"'Ah me!' said the giant, 'I shall die of starvation.'

"'Don't, if you love me,' said Violet.

"'Enough,' cried Growlegrum. 'Here lovely Princess is the first, and every day you shall have another.'

"So saying, he jerked a beautiful young lady out of his pocket and set her down inside of the castle.

"'Good-bye,' said the Princess.

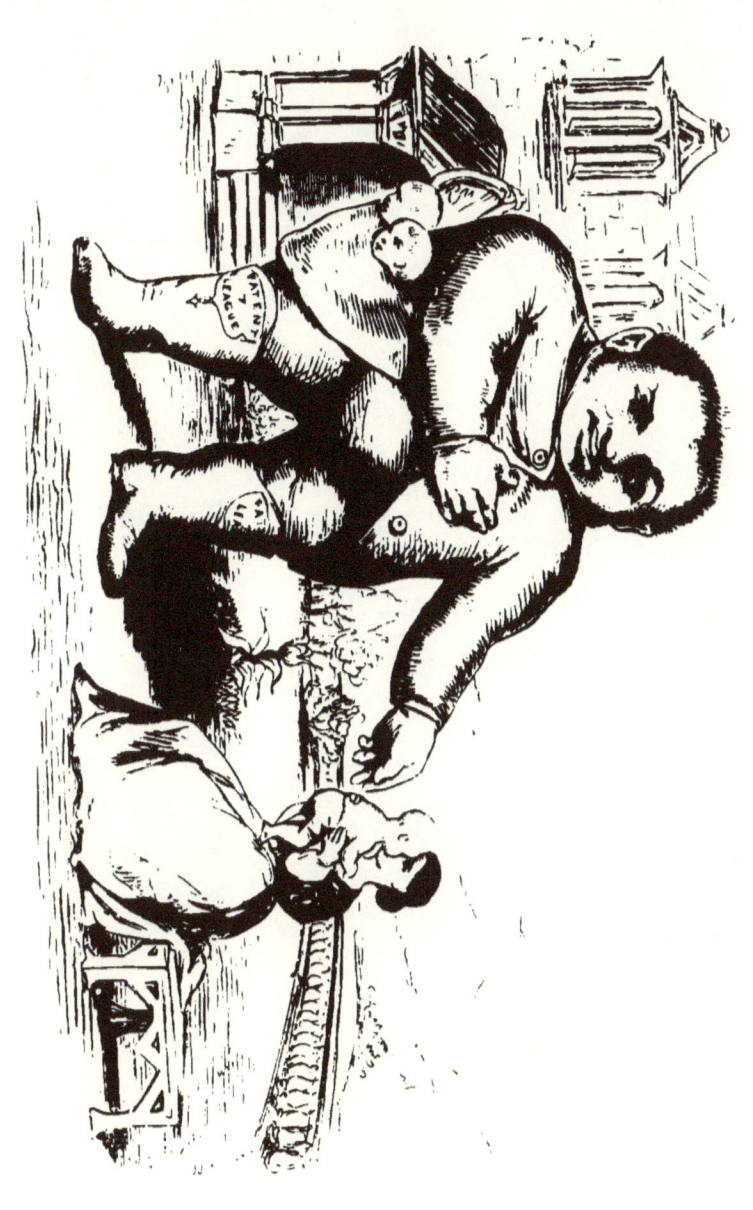

" ' Good-bye,' said the giant, ' If I stay I shall steal a baby.'

" So he gnashed his ugly grim teeth and walked away with vast steps.

" When he was out of sight Prince Bluets came forth, and the Princess and he laughed with joy, because of the babies whom they had saved. But as there was no time to lose the Prince kissed her and wriggled through the key-hole again.

" Then in haste he ran into the woods and took the road which led to the city where King Hassan lived.

" On the way he heard voices, and climbing a tree he listened eagerly until he learned that these came from five persons who were dressed in long robes and were riding from the town. By good luck they rested a little while just under the tree in which Bluets lay hidden. He soon understood that all five were lawyers whom the King had sent to see Krusstikuss, that they might offer the Princess in marriage to him with half of the kingdom if he would send his brother away, and learn to eat beef and mutton in place of babies.

" ' Ho !' said the Prince, ' This won't do,' so he waited till they left, and then descending ran back to the castle and called the Princess.

" Then through the key-hole he gave her a little advice about the five lawyers. After this he went away once more towards the city.

" As for the Princess she waved her handkerchief from the castle wall until Growlegrum espied her and strode over the hills and valleys to the castle.

" ' Sir,' she said, ' Do not be surprised if you see a party of men in gowns coming from the city. Go and meet them, if they think you are Krusstikuss they will tell you something.'

" ' Good,' answered he. ' Now I perceive that you love me.'

" Then, without waiting, he walked towards the city. A little way on he met the five lawyers. As soon as they saw him they dismounted and threw themselves on the ground.

" ' What do ye want?' roared Growlegrum.

" ' Oh sir !' said they, ' we would see the great giant Krusstikuss.'

" ' It is well,' returned the giant. ' Speak.'

" ' Sir,' said they, ' We come to offer to the great giant Krusstikuss one-half of the kingdom and the Princess for a wife.'

" ' Ha !' answered the giant, ' and what shall his brother have ?'

" ' Perhaps,' returned one of the lawyers, ' he might be persuaded to leave, or else your highness could quietly knock him on the head.'

" ' Scoundrels !' roared Growlegrum, ' My name is not Krusstikuss. I'll teach you to make trouble, you rascals.'

"Upon this he seized them one after another, and ate the whole five. The effects of this meal were dreadful. In five minutes Growlegrum was bent double with stomach-ache, for you see the lawyers disagreed with him, and they also disagreed with one another inside of him.

"But this was not all, for in a few moments he began to grow so quarrelsome that he became the most unsafe giant that could anywhere be found.

"In half an hour he was outrageous, and by the time he met his brother he was ready to fight anybody.

"Well the end of it was they did fight. They fought for two days and two nights, when Krusstikuss got so weak that Growlegrum took him up by the heels and stood him on his head and gave him a mighty spin, for he was made just like a top, and then, while he was spinning, treated him to a kick, and hoisted him over two hills into the sea, where he spun to the bottom and never more was heard of.

"When this awful battle was over Growlegrum sat on a hill and began to pick his teeth with a fence rail. Meanwhile Prince Bluets hastened to the city.

"He had gone but a little way when who should he see but his great-great-grandfather Jack, the Giant Killer, who had journeyed a long way to see what had become of Bluets. After they had embraced one another, the Prince told his grandfather all that had passed.

"'You have done well,' said Jack, 'but we must now

get rid of this other giant who I hear is a terrible fellow. Let us go and see him.'

"'Very well,' replied Bluets, 'We will go,' and so saying they turned, and very soon spied Growlegrum sitting on the hill. As soon as ever he saw them he roared out,

"'Dinner! Here comes my dinner!'

"When they had come still nearer Jack cried aloud, 'I am Jack, the Giant Killer, and I have come to visit you.'

"'Ha, ha!' laughed the giant, 'You are a little man and brave.' 'There is one thing you cannot do, big though you be,' said Jack.

"'Name it,' said Growlegrum. 'I can pull up trees and kick down towns and chew cannon balls and eat you. What is there I cannot do?'

"'Sir,' answered Jack, 'All these things are easy.' 'If I cannot eat anything and kill anybody I will quit this land and go home,' said the giant in a rage.

"'Good!' cried Jack, 'Come with us.'

"Upon this the giant picked them both up and walked off in the direction which Jack pointed out. Presently they came to a house.

"'Stop!' said Jack, and the giant set them down.

"'Eat the man who lives in that house,' said Jack.

"'Poh!' cried Growlegrum, and gave the house a kick which knocked it down in a twinkling. Then he pulled out of the ruins a man who began to roar for mercy.

"'Oh dear!' he said, 'Don't eat me, and I will never fib any more, and never make any more speeches ever again.'

"'Who is he?' asked the giant. 'A *member of Congress*,' cried Jack.

"'Eat *him?* eat *him?*' said the giant, 'I don't want to be poisoned. You must think I am a fool.'

"'Eat him!' cried Jack.

"'No, sir,' said Krusstikuss. 'I'd rather leave. If I must die I would like to die easy.'

"So saying the giant gave a groan and set off across the hills. I do not know where he went, but I suppose he travelled home to his mamma, and told her what a fool Jack had made of him.

"As soon as the giant had gone Jack and Prince Bluets went to the castle and set free the Princess and all the babies, who showed their gratitude by screaming for a week. But perhaps this might have been owing to the dough-nuts they had eaten.

"I do believe there never was such a wedding as that of Prince Bluets and Princess Violet, for all the fairy folk came, and Cinderella and all the fairy godmothers, and Aladdin, and Prince Nosey, and the seven champions, and Hop O'my Thumb, Goody Two Shoes, and Red Riding Hood. All of them brought presents to the bride, but the Prince gave her only his love and took away from

6

her the amulet for fear it should make any one love her
more than he could."

During the next week it rained so hard every day
that no one of the spider's family could venture out of
their den.

It was no wonder that they became hungry for stories, and that at the first gleam of sunshine they all ran
together and began to pull at the line of cobweb to which
poor Fuz-Buz was fettered.

As for Fuz-Buz he was so wet and cold that he crawled
out of his hole with trouble and pain.

"Ah, my dears!" cried he. "I ache all over with the
gout. We lived too high in Spain I fear."

"Bother the gout!" said the spiders.

"Tell us a new story, and pretty soon too, or mammy
will eat you, and won't that be worse than the gout?"

"I don't know," answered Fuz-Buz, "I think I would
rather be eaten up at once, and have it over."

"Ha! ha!" cried Mrs. Grabem, who overheard what
the fly had said.

"Ha! ha! you would like to be eaten; would you
like to have your legs pulled off and your wings torn,
and —— ?"

"Oh dear! oh dear!" shrieked Fuz-Buz. "Pray stop,
I am all in a shiver. I will never be so hasty again."

"Very well," returned the spider firmly. "See that

you remember what I have said, and on no account venture to keep my blessed little children waiting. It spoils their tempers for life. I will have no more of it."

When Mrs. Grabem ceased, all the young spiders cried aloud,

"You had better take care, or mammy will finish you?"

"How are your legs?" said one.

"Where is that story?" said another.

"Here it is," answered Fuz-Buz, tapping his head. "I have it all here ever since the day I heard it told by a famous Dervish at the porch of the great Mosque of Salamanca."

Mustapha, or the Musical Gourd.

"In the year of the Hegira, 709, and the twelfth of our Caliph Haroun, the Magnificent, there lived in the royal city of Bagdad a cobbler of the name of Ali Ben Slippah.

"His shop was small, but being well situated at the corner of the street of the Prophet, and the great street of Mosques, the cobbler managed to live very comfortably, so that with the aid of Smyrna tobacco and a contented disposition which the poet has well called the 'Pipe of the just,' he eked out a tranquil life free from care and ambition.

"His house was neatly kept by his daughter Lelie, or the Dark-eyed, who was a little maiden with lips like the roses of Istamboul, and cheeks as darkly lovely as the brown lilies of Ispahan.

"Besides these the sole remaining member of their household was a great black cat known by the name of Yussef, or the Hump-backed, because she was always in an evil humour, and was forever hunching her back up to show how cross she felt.

"It so chanced that when Lelie was a child this cat pursued by boys and dogs had taken refuge with Lelie, who had saved her life. Thenceforward she had never left her, but was so jealous of her mistress that it was enough to look at her to drive the Pussy crazy with rage.

"Now to let you into a secret. You should know that Yussef was a wicked genius who for a terrible crime had been condemned to live an hundred years in the body of a cat.

"About the time at which this true story begins, a young soldier of the Caliph's guard, whose name was Mustapha, fell in love with Lelie, and as he was very handsome and clever, was so lucky as to make her also love him in return.

"Unhappily for them both, Yussef overheard Mustapha speaking of the day when they were to be married, and at once fell into a fit of jealousy which was dreadful to see.

"In her wrath she flew at Mustapha and scratched his

nose, then knocked down and broke the cobbler's best chibouque, and at length dashed out of the house just as Ali Ben Slippah threw his lap-stone at her in fierce anger, because of his broken pipe.

"It was late in the evening when Yussef darted out, and with her heart full of jealous rage bounded up the walls and over the house-tops, until at last she seated herself on a gable and began to think.

"As it became later she was suddenly aware of a noble-looking person who was walking slowly along, followed at a short distance by four guards with drawn scimetars.

"As soon as Yussef saw the cavalier she knew that he was the Caliph, and remembering that he was then seeking everywhere for beautiful women to wait upon his sick daughter, she formed on the moment the most spiteful scheme of mischief that ever you heard of.

"With two or three crazy leaps she alighted at the feet of the Caliph and began to miaou a tune of the most singular character.

"'By the beard of the Prophet!' said Haroun al Raschid, 'This is passing wonderful! Catch that cat!'

"But Yussef was too quick for that. She turned two somersaults, and miaoued again. The guards and the Caliph followed her in wonder, while she retreated until they came to the cobbler's door. Here she miaoued once more, and leaped into an open window.

"When the Caliph drew near as she had desired he

6 *

would do, he looked into the window and saw the beautiful Lelie.

"'Bismillah!' cried he, as he thrust back the guards. 'Blessed be cats for evermore! Here is the maiden I have sought for my daughter.'

"So saying, he turned and gave brief orders to his attendants bidding them be careful and secret; and thus saying moved away quietly through the deserted streets.

"Very early next morning when the cobbler had gone to market Yussef heard a noise, and looking saw the shop full of black slaves who seized Lelie, muffled her in a shawl, and leaving a bag of gold on the counter hurried away swiftly.

"As soon as they left Yussef hastened after them, and when they entered a gilded caique on the Tigris, she also tried to leap into the boat. But to her dismay one of the guards seized her by the tail and threw her thirty feet away into the river.

"Yussef spluttered and spit as she came to the surface, and must surely have been drowned had she been a real cat.

"As it was she lost three out of her nine lives, and unluckily came to land on the premises of a tanner where she was set upon by six dogs who tore her hair out and bit her tail, and altogether so misused her that she came to look more like a bit of ill-used foot-rug than a respectable Maltese cat.

"At last, with her heart full of rage and her stomach full of water, she reached home to find the poor cobbler in the utmost grief for the loss of his daughter.

"By and by he resigned himself to his fate, and seeing well that no common person had stolen the maiden, he smoked the more abundantly, and like a true believer took comfort in that verse of the Koran which says, 'All things that are are well; but some, saith the Prophet, are disagreeable.'

"Meanwhile poor Mustapha became nearly crazed with grief. He roamed the streets all day, and at evening returned to the cobbler's in the vain hope of hearing some news of Lelie.

"On one of these occasions he was so unlucky as to stumble over Yussef who gave him a fierce scratch, and fled from his wrath to devise new plans of mischief, for although Lelie was gone, she was lost to herself as well as to Mustapha, and the cat never had ceased to hate him as the cause of all her troubles.

"Yussef therefore resolved to rid herself of his presence, and she set about it after her own wicked fashion.

"Some two or three nights later Mustapha was wandering sadly in the gardens of the Caliph when he heard a voice from the trees above him saying,

"'Come to-night to the tomb of the Caliphs, under the cedars, on the road to Damascus, and thou shalt hear news of thy love.'

"The voice sounded like that of Lelie, and the soldier in vain sought about him on every side for its source. At length the words were repeated and he made up his mind to obey them.

"It was near midnight when Mustapha found himself at the appointed spot. All Bagdad lay behind him still and slumbering. Here and there a long arrow of light darted from some tall minaret, while the full moonlight pouring down on the Mosque of El Rahab lit up its golden dome like a mound of fire.

"Before him the quiet groves of fig and olive, pomegranates and mourning cypresses stretched away for miles, bounded in the far distance by the curves of the Tigris, whose broad bendings flashed in the light like gigantic scimetars.

"As Mustapha approached the Caliph's tomb he came to an open space girt in by dense thickets. Pushing these aside he stepped cautiously forward, for he heard a sound of music and voices.

"Presently a fire flashed up on the open ground among the ruined tombs, and the soldier shook with fear as he looked on what its light revealed.

"Seated about the slope which led downwards on every side to a broken tomb were gigantic figures in white robes that floated about them like mist, so that only sometimes he could see their solemn faces.

"From the tomb came slowly a long procession of

Ghouls and Vampires and Afrites of hideous shapes, such as men see in dreams, while all the air and the ground seemed to be alive with a myriad of little winged forms who hovered about like butterflies.

"At last there was silence, when Yussef suddenly appeared before the tallest of the Genii, and miaoued frightfully.

"Then the Genie said in a mild great voice, 'What would you of your brethren?'

"'The man,' said Yussef, 'who has mocked my fallen estate and stolen my love from me is here awaiting judgment.'

"When Mustapha heard these words he was ready to die with fear, but his limbs refused to bear him away and he was forced to support himself by grasping a tree.

"'Oh King,' cried Yussef, 'Let him be brought to thee.'

"'Be it so!' said the Genie.

"At this two fearful-looking Afrites leaped into the air, and with one swoop of their clawed wings alighted beside Mustapha. Then they seized him and thrust him into the circle before the cloudy form of the King of the Genii who thus addressed him.

"'It is not given us to slay, but that thou shalt no more trouble us we order thee to become a gourd, and as we may not sentence any to an endless fate it shall be that when it pleaseth Allah to turn thee inside out thou shalt then only assume again the form of man.'

"'It is well,' cried Yussef. 'Thanks, oh King!'

"At these words Mustapha fainted. When he recovered he found himself hanging on a vine near by, and presently discovered that he was a huge green gourd.

"After this many days fled away, and Mustapha the gourd grew bigger and bigger, and at last began to ripen and turn yellow.

"Every night as he hung on the vine he saw the strange midnight meetings of the Genii and Ghouls and Afrites. All the wonderful things he heard and saw no one will ever know, for he saw their wild feasts and dances, and heard music such as before no mortal ears had ever listened to.

"At length one warm summer morning two farmers came by on the way to market.

"'Bismillah!' cried one, as he saw the great gourd Mustapha. 'What a monstrous gourd!'

"'Let us take it with us and sell it,' said the second.

"Thus saying he took a knife from his girdle and cut the stem by which Mustapha hung. This caused him so much pain that he cried aloud,

"'What's that?' said the farmer. 'The gourd speaks! It is alive!'

"Upon this he pricked the gourd with his knife. At this Mustapha exclaimed, 'Don't!'

" ' Mahomet !' said the farmer. ' The thing is enchanted. It will fetch us a fortune.'

" Shortly afterwards they carried the gourd to the market. Here they made a goodly fortune by running pins into Mustapha that he might cry out for the amusement of the by-standers.

" Before long all Bagdad flocked to see and hear this wonderful gourd, and at last an officer of the Caliph's household arrived, payed a great sum for the gourd, and putting it in a basket, carried it away to the Palace.

" By and by Mustapha found himself in a superb room of the Palace, where, surrounded by her ladies, the Princess lay upon a couch.

" Suddenly Mustapha the gourd as he lay in his basket heard the voice of his beloved Lelie who was fanning the Princess.

" This so moved poor Mustapha that he cried aloud,

" ' Allah ! I hear my love !' and so saying rolled from the basket and fell at Lelie's feet.

" ' Mahomet !' cried the Princess. ' The thing is bewitched ! take it away !'

" But as for Lelie the words were as sweet music to her, and seizing the gourd she placed it tenderly in the basket and carried it to her room. Here she implored it with tears to speak again, but in vain ; so that at last she was forced to leave it and return to the Princess.

" Soon after she had gone Mustapha was aware of a

rose-colored cloud in the room, out of which grew into shape the form of a huge Genie which thus addressed him.

" 'Know, frail mortal, that I am your guardian spirit. I have heard with pity of your sad fate and am come to give you a chance for life again. Perhaps what I shall do for you may render your position better. Unluckily I cannot give to you once more your mortal shape.'

"With these words the figure inclined towards him gravely and touched his yellow cheek. He shuddered and lost consciousness.

"What next was his amazement to find himself standing in the shop of Harim, the merchant. Presently he began to look at himself with curious care. He had a gold head like that of a bird, with ruby eyes. His neck was of satin wood, long and slim, while his clothes which were stiffened with whalebone and wire, resembled petticoats upside down.

" 'Allah il Allah !' cried he, 'What an existence !'

"Just then a Dervish looking at him asked the merchant, 'What is that?'

" 'It is,' answered he, 'a Frankish device which the men in Frangistan carry to keep off the rain. Their women are only allowed to carry smaller ones, so they make up for that by bearing them about in fair as well as wet weather.'

" ' A device of Eblis !' exclaimed the Dervish, and muttering a verse of the Koran, walked gravely away.

" By and by came the grand Purveyor of the Caliph. He was seeking new and curious things for the Princess, who was ill and refused to eat so that day after day she became more feeble.

" ' Ah !' said the Purveyor, ' This is a Frank tent. I saw them when I was Envoy to the court of Charlemagne.'

" At this Mustapha blushed, for the officer seized him and began to expand his skirts so that his leg, for he had but one, was alarmingly exposed.

" Very soon the Purveyor, having paid a good price, took Mustapha away to the Palace where he explained the uses of this portable tent.

" ' This,' said he, ' Is what the Franks, whom Allah confound ! call an umbrella, and the female of the thing they term a parasol.'

" ' I shall need it not,' said the Princess Ellera. ' No sun will shine on me any more. On me no rain will fall. I shall die if I find nothing that I can eat.'

" ' Take it Lelie,' she cried, ' As thou hast lost thy gourd, take it.'

" Upon this Lelie took Mustapha away and placed him in a quiet corner of her room.

" Meanwhile some days went by, and all the cooks tried in vain to please the sick Princess. All day long

an army of slaves went past her bed, each bearing some
rare dish or some luscious fruit, but still alas! in vain;
so that at length the doctors decided that if she did not eat
within a day she would surely die.

"Lelie, who was in great distress, left the Princess and
went to her own room to weep alone. At last she arose
to go out into the garden, thinking that perhaps the
Princess might be tempted by a rose-leaf salad.

"As she walked past Mustapha he cried aloud, 'Take
me.'

"'This is queer,' said she, but when the words were
repeated she clutched the Frankish toy and ran out into
the garden. Here she wandered long, but as evening
fell she suddenly saw that a storm had gathered.

"Before she could reach the Palace, a wild gust of
wind caught in Mustapha's skirts and nearly tore him
from her hand. As she struggled the wind expanded his
petticoats, and at last crack went the wires, and then
what do you think?

"Mustapha was turned inside out, and the umbrella
was a man once more.

"In a moment he explained everything, but after he had
kissed her twice she began to sob, for now she knew that
he had escaped one evil fate only to light upon another as
fearful. "'Ah!' she cried, 'a man! You, a soldier, in the
gardens of the Palace! You will be put to death at
once.'

" 'No !' he answered, after thinking a little. 'Not if I can save the Princess. Let us go to the Caliph and confess all. Meanwhile have no fears.'

" Lelie at last gave her consent, and with trembling steps she left him, and seeking the Princess related their strange story.

" In a moment all was confusion. A man in the harem !

" 'Bowstrings and sacks !' cried the captain of the guard, as he hurried Mustapha before the Caliph.

" 'Wretch !' said Al Raschid the Caliph, 'Who art thou ?'

" 'A soldier,' said Mustapha.

" 'Let him die !' cried Al Raschid.

" 'Oh Caliph,' answered Mustapha, 'In the land of the Genii it was given me once to learn secrets of the vile Franks, wherewith it may be that I can save thy daughter the Princess.'

" 'Thou dost lie like unto a rusty weathercock,' said the Caliph, 'But that none may say I am unjust, take this man to the kitchen. Let him do his best, and if he fail have him strangled instantly.'

" 'It is well said,' replied Mustapha.

" Very soon he was left alone in the great kitchen of the Palace, while all the strange things he had seen at the feasts of the Genii came back to his mind.

" Presently he sought about him among the stores of

provisions, and took from a basket those striped apples which grow by the brooks of Alkeldrina.

"These he pared deftly and set each within a cup of wheaten dough, such as only the Caliph's farms can furnish. Therein he placed also the golden orange-peel and the spices of distant Borneo. Lastly, he sprinkled it within and without with the aromatic sugar of Turkan, and hanging each apple thus prepared in a silken net carefully cooked them.

"When they were ready he placed them upon golden dishes, and threw over each a hail of snowy sugar and fragrant cinnamon, covering all with a handful of almond blossoms.

"Then he called the guard, and with scimetars crossed over his head he was allowed to carry his dish to the Princess. As she looked languidly upon it he shook off the blossoms.

"'Then,' said the Princess, 'These be the roses of Paradise which I do smell.'

"At these words he knelt down and offered the dish to the lady. Wonderful to tell the Princess called for a silver fork and ate up the whole of the apples so greedily that she scalded her throat in the most dreadful way.

"But between every mouthful she blessed poor Mustapha as the king of cooks, and from that instant she recovered so quickly as to disgust all the doctors, who said Mustapha was a quack, and went away.

"Of course he married Lelie, and had a patent for making this wonderful dish, and was created Lord Marquis of Apple-butter and Duke of Dumplings, and lived merrily all his days."

"That's a good story," cried the spiders.

"Glad you like it," said Fuz-Buz. "Now if you please I will sleep, as I am tired."

In this pleasant way the days went by until Fuz-buz had told them nine hundred and ninety-nine stories.

On this last evening he overheard the spiders talking as he lay tied by the leg in a deep dark crack of the apple tree where he slept.

"My children," said the old spider, "After Fuz-Buz has told us one more story we will eat him. It will be best to wait until after dark, and then seize him on a sudden and kill him; for he is a very strong fly, and may give me trouble."

They all agreed to this excepting the youngest, who said it would be a shame to serve him so, and that they ought to let him go.

But Mrs. Grabem replied, "You know nothing of house-keeping my dear. Go to sleep and hold your tongue."

When Fuz-Buz overheard all this he was scared to death. All next day he was so sick that he could not even tell the shortest story.

7 *

At night-fall when the family had gone to their den, he sat on the tree near his cosy little crack and tried to gnaw the web which held him.

Unluckily it was too tough. When he was in despair who should hum by but a huge Bee.

"Halloa!" said he, "What's wrong with you?"

"Sir!" replied Fuz-Buz, "I am tied by the leg to this web, and am to be eaten to-night by a cruel monster of a spider who lives near, and who will overhear you if you do not speak in a low voice."

"Who's afraid?" said the Bee. "Which leg is it?"

"This," answered Fuz-Buz.

"Pshaw!" cried the Bee, and with that he twisted the web about his legs and gave a jump. Snap went the line and Fuz-buz was free once more. Never a fly was so glad as he.

"Sir!" he said, "I am only sorry that you have not had the honour to slay this vile spider. Now if you were to slip into this crack where I sleep, you would have a fine chance, because when Mrs. Grabem comes to eat me you could give her a pleasing surprise."

"That's a rather jolly notion," answered the Bee. So he went down on the ground, and after sharpening his sting on a smooth pebble, thrust himself deep into the crack where Fuz-Buz was wont to sleep.

But as for Fuz-Buz the fly, he sat on a limb above and looked on. After a little, when it was dark or nearly so, out came Mrs. Grabem slowly, and crawling over her web went down into the crack to murder poor innocent Fuz-Buz. Presently she cried aloud,

"Oh! I'm dead!" which was true in a moment, for Sir Bee had run his long sword straight through her, and she had tumbled off the tree as dead as could be.

At the sound of her voice all the young spiders ran out, and in a moment they saw Sir Bee with his quick sword. In a twinkling he stabbed them one after another, until he came to the youngest. Then Fuz-Buz said,

"Halloa! my friend, let this one go, for he was the only one who did not desire to kill me."

"Sir!" cried the youngest spider, "I do not wish to live after you have killed my mother and all my brothers and sisters. Take that, sir!"

So saying he dealt the Bee such a crack that he was forced to stab him like the rest, and there at last was the end of all of them.

As for Fuz-Buz he said "Well, it's one spider less, and so many flies more. Spiders are of no use and flies are."

Meanwhile Sir Bee wiped his sword and took up his bag of honey, feeling that he had done a clever day's work, while Fuz-Buz flew away to Spain, and never could be brought to tell anybody a story long or short up to the end of his happy life.